OCKETA-POCKETA-POCKETA-WHEEEZE!-POCKETA-WHEEEEEEZE!

ZONDERKIDZ

The Berenstain Bears® The Bear Family Treasury

Requests for information should be addressed to:
Zonderkidz, *Grand Rapids, Michigan 49530*

ISBN 978-0-310-62037-2

The Berenstain Bears® God Bless Our Home ISBN 9780310720898
The Berenstain Bears® Play a Good Game ISBN 9780310712527
The Berenstain Bears® Love Their Neighbors ISBN 9780310712497
The Berenstain Bears® Get Involved ISBN 9780310720904
The Berenstain Bears® Jobs Around Town ISBN 9780310722861
The Berenstain Bears® and the Easter Story ISBN 9780310720874
The Berenstain Bears® Give Thanks ISBN 9780310712510
The Berenstain Bears® and the Joy of Giving ISBN 9780310712558

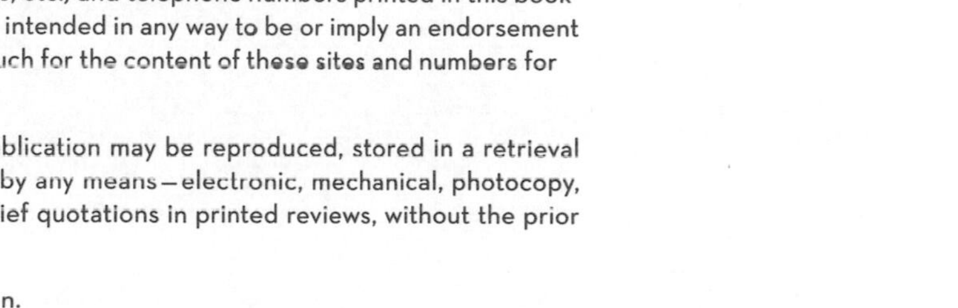

Editor: Mary Hassinger
Cover and interior design: Cindy Davis

Printed in China

13 14 15 16 17 18 19 /LPC/ 10 9 8 7 6 5 4 3 2 1

The Berenstain Bears®

Living Lights™

Bear Family Treasury

written by
Jan & Mike Berenstain

The Berenstain Bears®

God Bless Our Home

written by
Jan & Mike Berenstain

ZONDERVAN.com/
AUTHORTRACKER
follow your favorite authors

Living Lights™

ZONDERkidz

The Bear family, who lived down a sunny dirt road deep in Bear Country, loved their tree house home. They lived inside a great hollow, old oak tree. They moved there when Brother Bear was little from a cave way up in the mountains. That was before Honey or Sister Bear were even born.

The first thing that Mama Bear did when they moved into their new home was hang a framed sampler on the wall.

It said, “God Bless Our Home.”

"That's just what we need," said Papa. "God's blessings will make our new tree house into a happy home."

At first, the tree house had just a living room with a kitchen downstairs and two bedrooms upstairs. When Sister was born, she shared a bedroom with Brother. There was an attic nestled in the tree's thick upper branches too.

But the attic soon filled up with all the Bears' extra stuff—their chests of old clothes, unused baby carriages, and old-fashioned record players and radios. The tree house quickly started to seem a little cramped for a growing family. But then Papa set to work.

First, Papa dug a basement among the oak tree's great roots. That gave them plenty of room to store all their things.

Later, he built a garage for their car right next to the house. But Papa soon began to use the garage for his workshop and began parking the car in the driveway again.

All in all, the tree house was a fine place to live. The thick wood of the tree trunk kept them warm in the winter. The spreading oak leaves above kept the house shady and cool in the summer.

Brother and Sister loved to lie in bed in the evening and fall asleep to the sound of crickets and katydids in the branches outside. In the morning, they woke to the sound of a mockingbird singing his copycat song at their open window.

The Bears' tree house made a home for other creatures too. A woodchuck dug his burrow under the front steps. A family of chipmunks made their home in the woodpile.

A pair of sparrows nested in the birdhouse out back, and swallows built their nests of mud in the rafters of the garage. Papa had to duck when the swallows came swooping in to feed their babies. But he didn't mind.

"As the Good Book says," Papa explained, "'Even the sparrow has found a home, and the swallow a nest for herself.'"

The Bear family was very happy in their tree house. It's true, it was a little small. And when baby Honey came along, it suddenly seemed even smaller.

At first, Mama and Papa just put Honey's crib in their room alongside their bed. That was okay. While she was very small, Honey needed to be near them anyway.

But when Honey started to grow, it wasn't so fine. She started climbing out of her crib in the middle of the night and crawling into bed with Mama and Papa. She would sleep between them sideways and kick them in the stomach. Mama and Papa weren't getting enough sleep.

One morning, at breakfast, a sleepy Papa said to a sleepy Mama, "You know, maybe it's time we thought about moving to a bigger house."

"Mmm!" said Mama, half asleep. "Maybe you're right."

But Brother and Sister overheard them.

"Move to a bigger house!" they both said. "No way! We love our tree house!"

“We love it too,” said Mama. “But I’m afraid it’s getting too small for our growing family. Honey really needs a room of her own.”

“And there’s no garage for our car,” added Papa. “I have been parking in the drive for years now. When it snows, I have to shovel it out every time.”

“But there must be a way to make more room and keep living right here,” said Brother.

“Yes,” agreed Sister. “We just need to put on our thinking caps.”

“Maybe you’re right,” said Papa. “We probably could make more room somewhere.”

“Let’s look things over and see,” suggested Mama.

So the family took a tour of the tree house, inside and out, looking into every room, poking into every nook, and peering into every cranny. Papa got out his tape measure and made some notes. The family finished touring up in the attic. The Bears found a lot of things up there they hadn't seen in years.

“Look,” said Mama, “here’s my old trumpet from the Bear Country High School Marching Band.” She put it to her lips and blew a few notes. “I wonder if I can still play ‘Carnival of Venice.’” She tried it out. Brother and Sister put their hands over their ears.

“Mama!” they said. “Please!”

"I think I know what to do," said Papa, as they trooped down from the attic. "I can enlarge the basement and move some things down there from the attic. Then I can divide off part of the attic into a little room for Honey."

"That would work nicely," said Mama. "What about the car?"

"Simple," said Papa. "I'll just build a shed onto the side of the garage and park it in there. That will keep the car out of the snow."

"Yay!" yelled the cubs. "We can stay in our tree house. God bless our home!"

The next day, with the cubs' help, Papa set to work. They dug and carried and sawed and hammered, sanded, plastered, painted, and cleaned like a family of busy beavers.

Finally, after many days of hard work, it was all finished. Honey had a room of her own, and the family car had a place to sleep at night too.

"You know," said Papa, as he looked over their brand-new old home, "this isn't a bad little place, at that."

"Not bad?" said the cubs. "It's the best little place in the whole wide world!"

"Yes," said Mama, "and above all, it is our own home, sweet home." She pointed to the old framed sampler on the wall. "May God always bless our happy home."

PLAY a GOOD GAME

written by Jan and Mike Berenstain

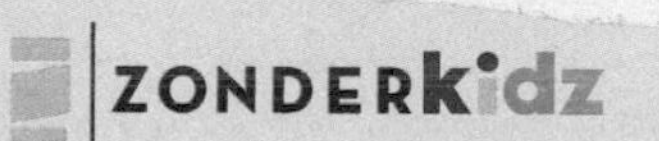

Brother and Sister Bear loved all kinds of sports. They played one sport or another all the year round.

But in the fall, when the leaves turned color and the first frosty nip was in the air, the thoughts of Brother and Sister Bear turned to ... soccer! They dusted off the old soccer ball and headed for the soccer field.

Their team was called the Rockets, and they did rocket around the field. They weren't the best team in the league, but they were pretty good.

Their coach was none other than Brother and Sister's own Papa Bear. He didn't really know that much about soccer. But he tried hard and was very good at cheering them on.

Brother and Sister tried hard too. The best players on the team were the Brunowsky twins, Bram and Bam. But Brother and Sister had their strong points.

Brother was a left-footed kicker. He was given the job of corner kicks from the right side. He was great at "bending" the ball in toward the goal.

Sister was a skillful "header." She could bop Brother's kicks right into the net with her head.

"My head is like a rock!" she said, rapping the top of her head with her knuckles.

"It sure is!" agreed Brother.

"Hey!" said Sister.

Brother and Sister didn't worry too much about winning. It was fun just to get out there and play.

"Remember, team," Papa always told them, "it's not whether you win or lose that counts, but how you play the game!"

There was one team, though, that didn't feel that way—the Steamrollers. Their best players were Too-Tall Grizzly and his gang. They were the schoolyard bullies of Bear Country, and they were big and tough and strong. They weren't very good soccer players, but that didn't matter. If you got in their way, they just ran over you.

Their coach was Too-Tall's dad, Two-Ton Grizzly. He was just as rough and tough as his son, only a whole lot bigger.

He said, "It isn't how you play the game that counts, but whether you win or lose!"

The Rockets' first game of the season was against the Steamrollers. Brother and Sister were definitely not looking forward to it.

"Don't worry," Coach Papa told his team. "Just play your best, and you'll all do fine!"

The players' families were in the stands to see the first game. Mama Bear was there with Honey Bear, of course. Grizzly Gramps and Gran were there too. Gramps was already whistling and cheering and stamping his feet.

"Come on, Rockets!" he yelled and, putting two fingers in his mouth, blew a whistle that you could have heard all over Bear Country.

"Now, Gramps!" said Gran. "Please control yourself."

"Aw, shucks!" he said. "Makin' a big fuss at a ball game is half the fun of rootin' for your team. It's all in good fun."

Brother and Sister were surprised to see that their Sunday school teacher, Missus Ursula, was in the stands. Missus Ursula had been the Sunday school teacher in Bear Country for a long, long time. She'd even taught Mama and Papa Bear when they were cubs.

Then, Brother and Sister remembered that Missus Ursula was the Brunowsky twins' grandmother. Bram and Bam waved to her as they ran onto the field.

The families of the Steamrollers were in the stands too. There was Too-Tall's mother, Too-Too Grizzly, and his big sister, Too-Much. Too-Much really was a big sister—she was almost twice Too-Tall's height. When she saw Brother, she waved and fluttered her eyelashes. She had a little crush on Brother. Brother just blushed.

The Steamrollers ran onto the field to warm up. They looked huge!

Brother and Sister looked at each other. They were going to get clobbered! Even Bram and Bam looked a little worried.

The referee blew his whistle, and the game began.

The Rockets had the ball, and Bram and Bam quickly brought it down the field, passing it expertly back and forth. Bram took the ball and headed for the goal.

"TAKE HIM OUT!" yelled Two-Ton from the sidelines.

Too-Tall came charging in like a water buffalo, slide-tackled Bram, and stole the ball. Bram went flying head over heels.

"Foul!" yelled Coach Papa.

But the referee shook his head. "He was going for the ball—no foul!"

"Going for the ball!" muttered Papa under his breath. "He was going for the ball right through my player!"

Too-Tall and his gang hustled the ball down the field and quickly scored a goal.

"How you like that one, shorty?" Too-Tall sneered at Bram as he trotted off the field.

"That's enough of that!" said the referee. "Play soccer!"

"Talk about poor sportsmanship!" muttered Papa.

The Rockets had the ball again. But the same thing happened. The Steamrollers just steamrollered them, scoring one goal after another. At halftime, the score was Steamrollers, five; Rockets, zero.

Coach Papa gave them a pep talk. "Don't let it get you down!" said Papa. "You're playing a good, clean game! The Steamrollers don't play fair. All they're interested in is winning, and they don't care how they do it. You wouldn't want to win that way, would you?"

"No," said Bram.

"But," said Bam, "it would be nice to score just one goal."

"I know how!" said Brother, getting an idea. "Let's set up a corner kick."

"Yeah!" said Sister. "They don't know that Brother kicks left footed. Maybe we can fool them!"

So the Rockets tried it. The next time they had the ball, Bam kicked it off Too-Tall's leg on purpose, and it went out of bounds. That set up the corner kick.

Carefully, Brother placed the ball in the right corner and kicked it hard with his left foot. The ball curved beautifully. Sister was right there. She leaped straight up, tipped her head, and bopped the ball into the goal! The score was now five to one.

But as Sister came down, Too-Tall charged her. He plowed into her and knocked her flat. Sister saw stars circling around her head and heard little birds chirping.

"Wha' happened?" she asked.

"Too-Tall happened!" said Brother, helping her up. "Are you okay?"

"I think so," said Sister, standing up. "Yeah, I'm all in one piece." Sister was a tough little cub.

Brother looked around for Too-Tall. He was so mad he was going to run right through him. But the referee had Too-Tall over to one side and was handing him a red card. Too-Tall was getting thrown out of the game for unnecessary roughness.

"WHAD'YA MEAN—UNNECESSARY ROUGNESS?" bellowed Coach Two-Ton, running out onto the field.

Two-Ton and the referee stood nose-to-nose, hollering at each other.

"Uh-oh!" said Brother. "Here comes Papa!"

Coach Papa came running onto the field too.

"That was my daughter who got unnecessarily roughed, you big lummox!" he yelled at Two-Ton. Now the referee was trying to keep them apart.

The stands emptied. Everyone ran onto the field. The players watched in amazement as Mama and Grizzly Gramps and Gran tried to drag Papa away while Too-Too and Too-Much Grizzly tried to hold Two-Ton back. Everyone was shouting and shoving and name-calling.

That's when a slim, slightly bent figure walked slowly onto the field. The crowd quieted down. A few of them took off their hats.

It was their Sunday school teacher, Missus Ursula.

"Now, Papa Bear," she said sternly. "And you too, Two-Ton Grizzly."

"Yes, Missus Ursula?" they said meekly.

"I'm very disappointed with both of you," she said, shaking her head. "Is this the way I taught you to behave in my Sunday school?"

"No, Missus Ursula," mumbled both coaches, hanging their heads.

"Is this any sort of example to set for the cubs?" she asked.

"No, Missus Ursula," they said.

"Well, then," she said. "Remember, 'Blessed are the peacemakers, for they will be called sons of God.' Now, let's see you two shake hands and finish the game."

So Papa and Two-Ton shook hands. Everyone took their seats, the referee blew his whistle, and the game went on.

For the rest of the game, no one heard a peep out of Coach Two-Ton or Coach Papa. The Steamrollers scored one more goal, and the Rockets scored two. The final score was six to three. Everyone played fair and had a lot of fun ... whether they won or lost.

After the game, both teams got together and went out to dinner at the Burger Bear.

Too-Much Grizzly sat next to Brother and fluttered her eyelashes at him. Brother just blushed and munched away on his double cheeseburger.

The Berenstain Bears®
Love
Their Neighbors
written by Jan and Mike Berenstain
Living Lights™
ZONDERkidz

The Bear family was quite proud of their handsome tree house home, and they worked hard to keep it neat and tidy. The trim was freshly painted, the front steps were scrubbed, and the windows were washed. The lawn was mowed, and the flower beds were weeded. Even the leaves of the tree were carefully trimmed and clipped.

Most of their neighbors took good care of their homes as well. The Pandas across the street were even bigger neatniks than the Bears. It seemed they were always hard at work sweeping and cleaning.

Farmer Ben's farm just down the road was always in apple-pie order too. Even his chicken coop was as neat as a pin.

"A place for everything and everything in its place, that's my motto," said Farmer Ben.

The Bear family had a few neighbors whose houses were positively fancy—like Mayor Honeypot, the bear who rode around Bear Town in his long lavender limousine. His house was three stories tall and built of brick. It had a big brass knocker on the front door and statues of flamingos on the front lawn.

Even more impressive was the mansion of Squire Grizzly, the richest bear in all Bear Country. It stood on a hill surrounded by acres of lawns and gardens. Dozens of servants and gardeners took care of the place.

The Bear family was proud of their neighborhood, and they got along well with all their neighbors.

Except for the Bogg brothers.

The Bogg brothers lived in a run-down old shack not far from the Bear family's tree house—but what a difference! Their roof was caving in, and the whole place leaned to one side. There was junk all over the yard. Chickens, dogs, and cats ran everywhere. A big pig wallowed in the mud out back.

"Those Bogg brothers!" Mama would say whenever she saw them. "They're a disgrace to the neighborhood!"

"Yes," agreed Papa. "They certainly are a problem."

One bright spring morning, the Bear family was working outside, cleaning up and fixing up, when the Bogg brothers came along. They were driving their broken-down old jalopy. It made a terrific clanking racket.

As they drove past the tree house, one of the Bogg brothers spit out of the car. It narrowly missed the Bears' mailbox.

"Really!" said Mama, shocked. "Those Bogg brothers are a disgrace!"

"I agree," said Papa, getting the mail out of the mailbox. "I'm afraid they're not very good neighbors."

Papa looked through the mail and found a big yellow flier rolled up. He opened it and showed it to the rest of the family.

"Oh, boy!" said Sister and Brother. "It's like a big block party! Can we go?"
"It certainly sounds like fun," said Mama. "What do you think, Papa?"
"Everyone in town will be there," said Papa. "We ought to go too."
"Yea!" cried the cubs.

So, on Saturday morning, they all piled into the car. They had a picnic basket and folding chairs. They were looking forward to a day of fun and excitement.

But, as they drove along, the car began to make a funny sound. It started out as a Pocket-pocketa-pocketa! But it soon developed into a Pocketa-WHEEZE! Pocketa-WHEEZE!

"Oh, dear!" said Mama. "What is that awful sound the car is making?"

Just then, the car made a much worse sound—a loud CLUNK! It came to a sudden halt, and the radiator cap blew off. They all climbed out, and Papa opened the hood.

"I guess it's overheated," said Papa, waving at the cloud of steam with his hat.

"Oh, no!" said Sister. "How are we going to get to the Bear Town Festival?"

"Maybe someone will stop and give us a hand," said Papa hopefully. "Look, here comes a car. Let's all wave. Maybe they will stop."

It was Mayor and Mrs. Honeypot in their long lavender limousine. They were on their way to the festival too. Their car slowed down, but it didn't stop. The mayor leaned his head out of the window.

"Sorry, we can't stop!" he said. "We're late already. I'm Master of Ceremonies today. I've got to be there on time. I'm sure someone will stop to help you."

And he pulled away with a squeal of tires.

"Hmm!" said Papa. "Maybe someone else will come along."

Soon, another car did come along. It was Squire and Lady Grizzly being driven to the festival in their big black Grizz-Royce. They slowed down too. Lady Grizzly rolled down her window.

"I'm afraid we can't stop," she said. "We don't have time. I am the judge of the flower-arranging contest. We simply must hurry."

And with that, they pulled away.

"Maybe no one is going to stop," said Sister. "Maybe we're never going to get to the festival."

"One of our neighbors is sure to stop and help us," said Mama. "After all, that's what neighbors are for."

"Yeah," said Brother. "But do *they* know that?"

A cloud of dust appeared down the road.

"Here comes someone now!" Sister said eagerly.

The dust cloud drew closer, and they could hear a clackety racket getting louder.

"Uh-oh!" said Papa, shading his eyes and peering down the road. "If that's who I think it is ..."

It was!

It was the Bogg brothers.

They came clanking up in their rickety old jalopy and screeched to a halt. First one, then another, then another of the Bogg brothers came climbing out.

"Howdy!" said the first Bogg brother.

"Hello, there," said Papa.

"I'm Lem," said the first Bogg brother. "I can see yer havin' some trouble with your ve-hicle."

"Well, yes, we are," said Papa.

"Maybe we can give you a hand," said Lem.

"That would be very neighborly of you," said Papa.

"Hey, Clem! Hey, Shem!" called Lem. "Git out the rope!"

The other two Bogg brothers rooted around in the back of the jalopy and came up with a length of rope. They hitched it to the back bumper of their car and tied the other end around the front bumper of the Bears' car.

"All aboard!" said Lem. The Bear family climbed hastily back in their car. The Bogg brothers pulled away, towing the Bears' car behind them.

"Where are they taking us?" asked Mama.

Papa shrugged. "At least we're moving!"

Brother and Sister hoped the Bogg brothers weren't taking them down to their old shack. They didn't want to meet that big pig.

They soon pulled into a run-down old filling station. Someone who looked like an older version of the Bogg brothers came out.

"Hello, Uncle Zeke," said Lem.

"Hello, Nephew," said Uncle Zeke. "What can I do you fer?"

"These poor folks broke down on the road," said Lem. "You reckon you can fix them up?"

"Let's take a look," said Uncle Zeke.

He looked under the car's hood, banged and clanged around, and came up with a length of burst hose.

"Radee-ator hose," he said. "Busted clean open. I should have another one of them around here somewheres."

Uncle Zeke rummaged around behind the filling station and soon came back with a radiator hose. He banged and clanged under the hood for a few more minutes.

“There,” he said, wiping his hands. “Good as new. We’ll top off the radee-ator, and you folks can be on your way.”

“Thank you very much!” said Papa, relieved. He shook hands with Uncle Zeke and the Bogg brothers.

"Thank you!" said Mama, Brother, and Sister. Honey Bear waved.
"How much do we owe you?" asked Papa, reaching for his wallet.
"Nothin'," said Lem. "This one is on us. After all, we're neighbors."

"That's right," said Mama with a gulp. "We are. In fact, how would you neighbors like to come over to our house for dinner next week?"

Papa, Brother, and Sister all stared at Mama with their mouths open.

"That's right neighborly of you," said Lem. "Don't mind if we do! Shem's cookin' has been getting a bit tiresome—too much possum stew."

"We were on our way to the Bear Town Festival," said Papa. "Would you like to join us?"

"Sure would!" said Lem. "We ain't been to a big shindig since Grandpap's ninetieth birthday party!"

So, the Bear family drove to Bear Town with the Bogg brothers and Uncle Zeke.

They were a little late, but they hadn't missed much … just Mayor Honeypot's welcoming speech. They all joined in the games, rides, and contests.

When it was time for the fireworks, the Bogg brothers livened things up with some music of their own.

The next week, the Bogg brothers came over to the Bears' tree house for dinner. They wore their best clothes and got all spruced up for the occasion. They even brought a housewarming gift: a big pot of Shem's special possum stew.

It was delicious!

The Berenstain Bears®
Get Involved
written by
Jan & Mike Berenstain
Living Lights™
ZONDERkidz

Brother and Sister Bear belonged to the Cub Club at the Chapel in the Woods. Preacher Brown was their leader. They did lots of fun things together. They went on picnics,

played baseball

and basketball,

sang in the chorus,
put on plays, painted
pictures of Bible stories,

and put up decorations in the chapel at Christmastime.

But the Cub Club was about much more than just doing fun things.

The real purpose of the club was to help others. There was always something that needed to be done around Bear Country. Sometimes it was cleaning up the Beartown playground.

Sometimes it was bringing food to bears who couldn't get out and about.

Sometimes it was even fixing up old houses for folks who couldn't fix them up themselves.

Brother and Sister liked to be helpful. It made them feel good deep down inside. Preacher Brown explained that it was always a good thing to help those in need.

"As the Bible says," he told them, "'Whoever is kind to the needy honors God.'"

So the Cub Club went right on helping others all over Bear Country.

Little did they know that very soon their help would be truly needed indeed!

One morning at breakfast, Papa Bear was reading the weather forecast.

"Says here it will rain for the next two days," he said. "Rain, rain, and more rain!"

"Oh, dear," said Mama. "I was planning to do laundry and air it out on the line. It will have to wait."

Brother and Sister didn't pay much attention. A little rain didn't seem to be anything to get very excited about.

On the way to school, Brother and Sister noticed the sky growing very dark.

By the time they reached school, it was starting to drizzle.

Through the morning, it rained harder and harder. It rained so hard that recess was cancelled and they had a study period instead.

"Phooey on rain!" muttered Brother.

"Rain, rain, go away," recited Sister. "Come again some other day."

But the rain paid no attention. It came pouring down harder than ever.

"I think you made it worse," said Brother.

When school let out, the cubs splashed their way home through the puddles. But then they heard a car coming down the road. It was Mama. She was coming to pick them up.

“Thanks, Mama,” said the cubs. “We were getting soaked!”

Back home, Papa had a fire going in the fireplace, and Mama spread their wet clothes out to dry. Brother and Sister played with Honey in front of the cozy fire.

"This rain is getting serious," said Papa. "There could be flooding along the river."

"Oh, dear!" said Mama. "That's where Uncle Ned, Aunt Min, and Cousin Fred live. I do hope they don't get flooded out."

Brother and Sister pricked up their ears. What would it mean if Cousin Fred's family got "flooded out"?

At bedtime, Brother and Sister could hear the wind howling and the rain beating against the windows. It was a little spooky, but they snuggled down under the covers and soon drifted off to sleep.

They dreamed about
rushing streams

and roaring waterfalls.

It was still raining when they woke up the next morning.

“Wow!” said Brother, pressing against the windowpane. “Look at it coming down!”

As Brother and Sister went downstairs, they heard Papa on the phone.

“Don’t worry,” he said. “I’ll be right over!”

“Over where?” asked Mama.

"That was Preacher Brown," said Papa, getting his coat and hat. "The river is rising fast, and we'll need to get everyone out of their houses down there. We're meeting at the chapel."

"We'll all come with you," said Mama. "There'll be plenty for everyone to do."

Brother and Sister were excited. They had never been part of a rescue mission before.

At the Chapel in the Woods, bears were gathering from all over. Their cars were loaded with shovels and buckets, bundles of blankets, and boxes of food. Grizzly Gus had a load of sandbags in his truck.

Preacher Brown saw Brother, Sister, and some of the other cubs. "I want all you Cub Club members to go along with your dads and help out," he told them. "This is what the Cub Club is all about!"

"Yes, sir!" they said. They were glad to be going. And Brother and Sister especially wanted to make sure Cousin Fred was all right.

The cars drove through the storm, down to the river.

"We're just in time," said Papa. "The water is nearly up to the houses."

An angry river was swirling over its banks and lapping toward the houses.

"Look! There's Cousin Fred!" said Sister.

Cousin Fred, with Uncle Ned and Aunt Min, was leaning out of an upstairs window and waving.

The bears all set to work piling up sandbags and digging ditches to keep the water away from the houses. Brother, Sister, Cousin Fred, and the rest of the Cub Club joined in. They dug and dug and dug until they were cold, wet, and tired.

Then everyone drove back to the chapel to warm up, dry off, and get something to eat.

Preacher Brown's wife, along with Mama and the other moms, had soup and sandwiches ready for all those cold, wet bears. They wrapped them in dry blankets and settled them down in the chapel's pews. Miz McGrizz sat at the organ to give them a little music.

"I'm so glad you're all right!" said Mama to Uncle Ned, Aunt Min, and Cousin Fred, giving them big hugs and kisses.

Preacher Brown got up in the pulpit, opened the Bible, and started to read: "The floodgates of the heavens were opened. And rain fell on the earth ... The waters flooded the earth ..."

Sister noticed a bright light coming through the chapel windows.

"Look!" she said. "The rain is stopping, and the sun is coming out!"

"The rain had stopped falling from the sky," read Preacher Brown.

"And there's a rainbow!" said Brother.

"I have set my rainbow in the clouds, ... " Preacher Brown read, and closed the Bible.

“With God’s help, we are all safe and sound,” said Preacher Brown. “Thanks to everyone for pitching in and helping out. I particularly want to thank our youngest helpers, the members of the Cub Club.”

All the bears clapped for Brother, Sister, Cousin Fred, and the Cub Club. They had been there to help others when their help was truly needed.

The Berenstain Bears®
Jobs Around Town
by Stan and Jan Berenstain
with Mike Berenstain
Living Lights™
ZONDERkidz

In Bear Country, there are many jobs to be done. Mama takes care of our tree house and family. Papa does chores and makes fine furniture to sell. But there are other jobs too. And if you pick the right job, work will be fun.

Let's take a trip around Bear Country and see what we might be when we grow up.

HONEY STO

Some jobs can be
exciting. We could fight
fires like Firebear Bob.

Or we could be policebears like Officer Marguerite. She tells us when to safely cross the road. If we don't obey, she blows her whistle …

We might be Beartown bus drivers. Or we might learn to drive a delivery truck, an ambulance, or even a cement mixer.

BEAR COUNTRY
AMBULANCE
AMBULANC
TRUCK CO.

Mama and Papa say God gives everyone a special talent. We can use our talent to do the job that is best for us and help others too.

Some folks are good at fixing things. They might be plumbers, mechanics, carpenters, or watchmakers. Almost everything we use sometimes has to have a fixer!

It would be fun to be a teacher and teach cubs how to read and write…

or a doctor and help make folks well.

We could have a store and sell good things like honey and bread.

Or we could work in a bank where money is kept safe and sound.

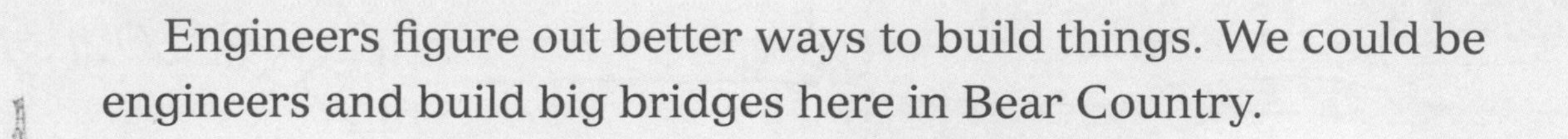

Engineers figure out better ways to build things. We could be engineers and build big bridges here in Bear Country.

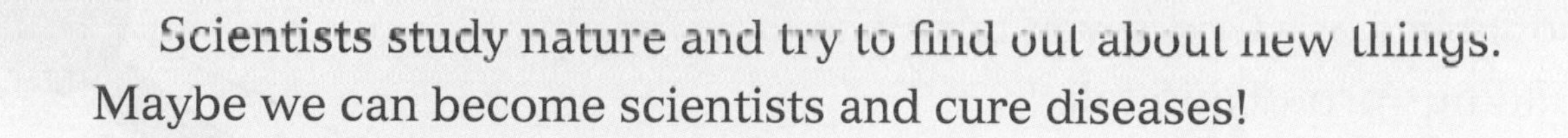

Scientists study nature and try to find out about new things. Maybe we can become scientists and cure diseases!

We could use our God-given talents to build buildings proud and tall.

Or we might be wreckers and tear down old unsafe buildings. That would be cool—POW!

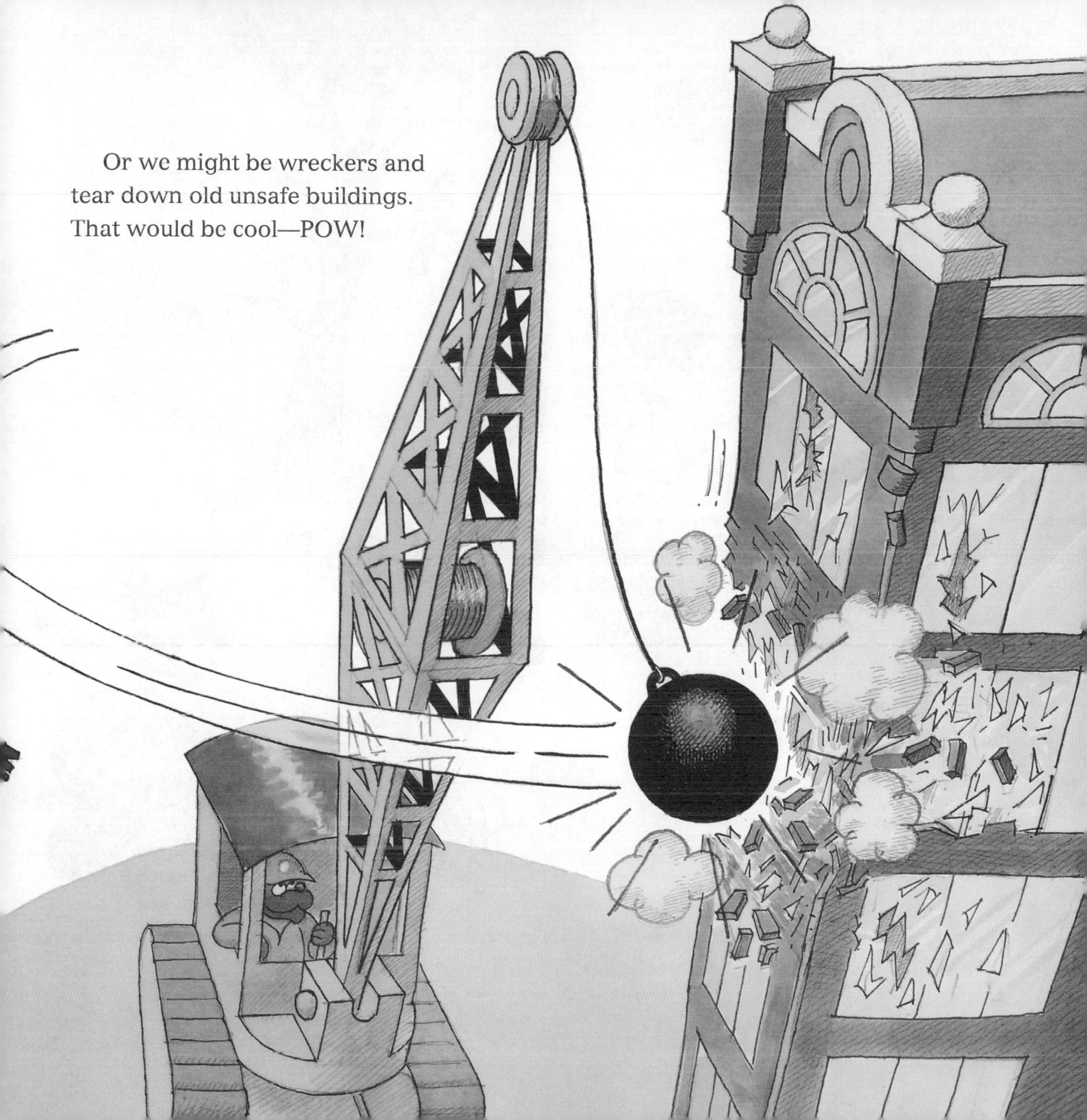

Brother, do you think my God-given talent is to be a singer? I've always loved to sing!

On second thought, I don't think I should. Maybe I don't really have a singing voice.

Don't worry, Sister, our job hunt is not over yet.

There are so many things to do and be. And the choice is up to you.

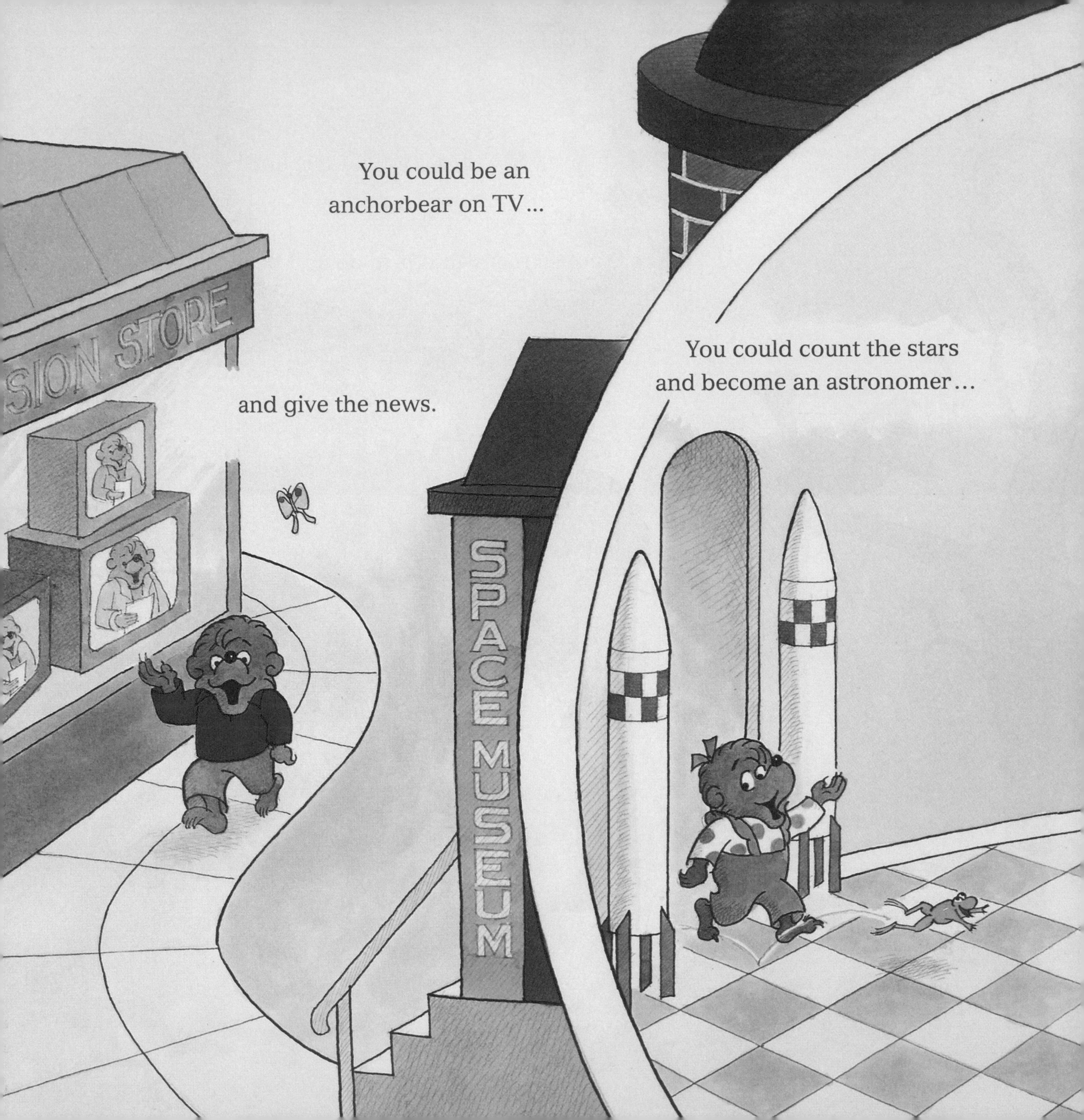

You could be an
anchorbear on TV...

and give the news.

You could count the stars
and become an astronomer...

or an astronaut and
visit distant planets
like Jupiter and Mars!

Hey, Sister! Look here. I love computer games. I could work with computers.

But I love Bear Country too. Being an environmentalist and helping stop pollution could be great.

You could be a beekeeper and work with beehives and honey. Mmmmm.

Say, I could be a carpenter like Papa Bear!

Forest rangers protect the trees by watching out for forest fires.

Or we could become farmers like our good neighbor, Farmer Ben.

Mr. and Mrs. Ben raise champion pigs. We could do that on our farm too. Our champion pig would be very, VERY big!

1ST PRIZE

As farmers, we could use God's good land to grow lots of food for all of Bear Country.

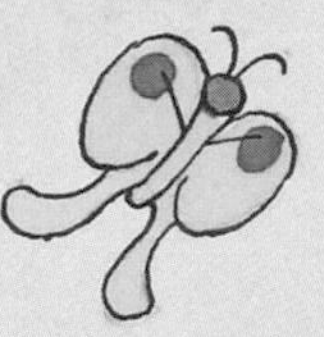

And, oh yes—a word of warning for future farmers: always watch out for the bull!

There are many things to do and be. It can be hard to choose. So if you haven't found the right thing for you ...

there's no need to worry. The job for you just may not have been invented yet!

So remember, there are many different kinds of work to choose from. And with God's help, you will pick the right job, help others everyday, and have fun too!

The Berenstain Bears®
and the
Easter Story
written by Jan & Mike Berenstain
Living Lights™
ZONDERkidz

It was springtime in Bear Country, and Brother, Sister, and Honey Bear were thinking about Easter. Actually, they were thinking about Easter candy. They loved Easter candy—there were so many different kinds! They were even thinking about it on their way to Sunday school one fine spring morning.

"My favorite Easter candy is chocolate bunnies," said Brother.

"My favorite is marshmallow chicks," said Sister.

"Jelly beans!" cried Honey Bear.

Their Sunday school teacher, Missus Ursula, overheard them. "I like the black jelly beans best," she smiled. "But, you know, there's much more to Easter than chocolate bunnies, marshmallow chicks, and jelly beans—black or otherwise."

"Sure, we know that," said Brother.

"Sure," said Sister.

"Sure!" said Honey.

"Oh?" said Missus Ursula. "Then why don't you tell the class all about Easter?"

"Well," said Brother, scratching his head, "it's about stuff in the Bible."

"Yeah," agreed Sister. "Bible stuff."

"Stuff!" nodded Honey.

"Hmmm," said Missus Ursula. "Maybe it's time we learned a little more about this 'Bible stuff.' It happens that the cubs in the next class are about to put on a play called *The Easter Story*."

"Can we watch, Missus Ursula?" the cubs asked.

"Just what I was about to suggest," she said.

Noah's Ark
David and Goliath

In the next classroom, everything was ready. Scenery was set up and the performers were in costume. One of them began to read the story out loud:

"Long ago, in the Holy Land, there was a man named Jesus. He traveled the countryside teaching about God and what God wanted for his people. Many listened to Jesus and followed him."

“Jesus was able to perform miracles. One time, he turned water into wine.

Another time he made a lame man walk. Jesus could do these wonderful things because he was the Son of God. He was called the Christ, which is a name for a king. But Jesus' kingdom is the kingdom of heaven."

“Jesus sometimes made people angry. Many people found his teachings strange, and some doubted that he was the Son of God. Others worried about why he was called ‘king.’ They were afraid that Jesus would become too powerful.”

"Jesus was from a small country town. But he traveled all the way to the Holy City of Jerusalem. One day, as he rode into the Holy City on a donkey, crowds of people greeted him. They shouted, 'Hosanna!' which means 'Save us!' The leaders of the city grew worried. Was Jesus becoming too powerful?

"One night, Jesus went to a garden to pray. While he prayed, soldiers were sent to arrest him. They took him away to prison."

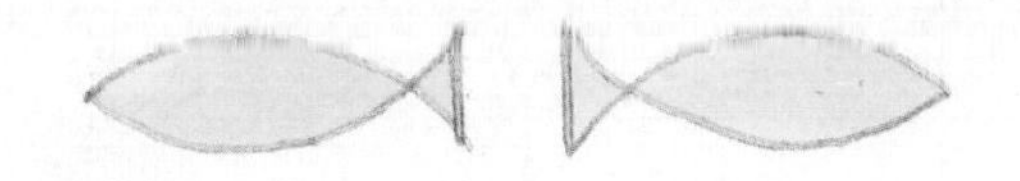

“Jesus was brought before a wicked judge. The judge asked Jesus many questions. He wanted to show everyone that Jesus was not a king. So he ordered Jesus to be put to death by hanging on a wooden cross.”

"The day Jesus died was a terrible day. The skies grew dark and a great wind arose. All the people were afraid."

“After Jesus died, his friends took him away. They put him in a tomb that was closed with a great stone.

Jesus was in the tomb for two days."

“On the morning of the third day after Jesus died, some women who knew Jesus came to weep at his tomb. They saw that the stone was rolled away and Jesus was gone. But an angel told the women not to be afraid. He told them that Jesus was alive once more.”

“Jesus came to visit his friends after he rose. They were amazed and fell down and worshiped him. Jesus told them they should spread the good news about what had happened.”

"Finally, Jesus rose up to heaven to be with God, his Father."

The play was over. Everyone was very quiet.

"Easter is about a lot more than candy, isn't it?" asked Sister.

"Yes, indeed," said Missus Ursula. "Are there any questions?"

"Yes," said Brother. "Does this mean we shouldn't eat any Easter candy?"

"Certainly not!" laughed Missus Ursula. "I wouldn't want to miss my black jelly beans either! It just means that on Easter morning, after you get your Easter baskets, you'll all go to church to learn more about Easter."

"Hooray!" the cubs said.

"And Hosanna!" added Missus Ursula. "He is risen!"

"Amen to that!" said Brother and Sister.

The Berenstain Bears Give Thanks

written by Jan and Mike Berenstain

It was autumn in Bear Country, and the sights and the sounds of the season were all around. The leaves on the trees were turning orange, red, and gold. There was a nip in the air, and the sky was a brilliant blue. Flocks of geese flew overhead honking their way south for the winter. Out in his cornfield, Farmer Ben was up on his big red tractor harvesting his crop.

Papa, Brother, and Sister Bear waved to him as they drove up the long drive to the farm. Papa was delivering some new furniture for Mrs. Ben. It was a fine new kitchen table and chairs.

Ben climbed down from his tractor and went to meet them at the farmhouse. Papa and the cubs unloaded the table and chairs and carried them inside. Mrs. Ben was pleased.

"My, don't they look nice!" she said. "It brightens the place up a bit. They do make my curtains look a mite shabby, though. I guess it's time I made some new ones."

"Thank you, Papa Bear," said Ben, shaking hands. "A job well done! Now, about our little deal ..."

The cubs wondered what "deal" Ben was talking about.

"I told you that you could have the pick of my produce in payment for the furniture," said Ben.

"That's right, Ben," said Papa as he nodded. "I was thinking of a few cases of your extra-special, grade-A, apple-blossom honey." Papa licked his lips just thinking about all that delicious honey.

"That's fine," agreed Ben. "You're welcome to it. And I have something else behind the barn that I think might interest you."

"Meet Squanto," said Ben, "my tom turkey. Isn't he a beaut?" Squanto was, indeed, a magnificent bird. He was enormous with a huge fanned tail and glowing colors of black, red, and gold.

"Wow!" said Papa, impressed. "That's some turkey!"

"He's beautiful!" said Sister. "But why is he called 'Squanto'?"

"That was the name of the Native Bear who helped the Pilgrims plant their corn when they settled in their new home," explained Ben. "Squanto celebrated the first Thanksgiving with them after their harvest. I couldn't think of a better name for a turkey."

"He sure is a fine bird," said Papa. "But what's he got to do with my furniture?"

"He's yours if you want him," said Ben. "He'll make you the best Thanksgiving dinner in all Bear Country."

Papa's eyes brightened. "Roast turkey—mmm-*mmm*!"

"Thanksgiving dinner?" said Sister, getting upset. "But that means ..."

"Now don't you fret, Sister Bear," soothed Ben. "Squanto can stay here till Thanksgiving. I'll fatten him up and deliver him all ready for your mama to cook on Thanksgiving morning.

"What do you say, Papa? Is it a deal?"

"It's a deal, Ben!" said Papa, and they shook hands on it. Papa was already imagining that mouth-watering Thanksgiving dinner—roast turkey with stuffing, two kinds of potatoes, gravy, green beans, and squash. Then dessert—pumpkin pie with whipped cream, and maybe some ice cream on top. Yum!

But Sister Bear wasn't so sure she liked the sound of all this. She had never met her Thanksgiving dinner before. It made things more personal. And Squanto was such a beautiful bird. She liked him a lot.

“You know, Papa,” she said as they drove home, “I don’t think having Squanto for Thanksgiving dinner is such a good idea. I think he would make a nice pet.”

“A pet?” said Papa in surprise. “Who ever heard of a turkey for a pet?”

“Why not?” asked Sister. “Lots of cubs have unusual pets. Barry Bruin has a raccoon. Lizzie Bruin has a goat. And Too-Tall Grizzly has a snake. Why couldn’t I have a turkey?”

Papa thought of that roast turkey Thanksgiving dinner with all the trimmings.

“Turkeys just don’t make good pets,” he said. “And that’s all there is to it!”

But Sister still didn’t like the idea of Squanto being a Thanksgiving dinner.

The weeks went past, and the leaves fell from the trees. The wind grew positively chilly, and one day, a few flakes of snow fell. Thanksgiving was drawing near.

Every day, Sister visited Squanto at the farm. He was growing fatter and finer. His feathers were bright and glossy. When he spread his tail, he looked like a big black, red, and gold peacock. But the closer it got to Thanksgiving, the sadder Sister got. She liked Squanto more and more each day.

Mama noticed that Sister was down in the dumps.

"You know, Sister," said Mama, putting her arm around her shoulder, "Papa's right—turkeys don't make very good pets. They aren't like dogs or cats. You can't play with them or run and jump with them. They're really just farm animals."

"I know," Sister sighed. "But I still like Squanto. He's so pretty."

Mama grew thoughtful. She saw that Sister was really serious about this.

"Now, dear, don't worry about it," she said. "Papa and I will talk it over and I'm sure we can work out something."

Sister brightened up. "Really?" she said. "You mean we won't have Squanto for Thanksgiving dinner?"

“We shall see what we shall see,” Mama said, smiling. “And, in the meantime, I have a surprise for you. I’ve been thinking we should make this Thanksgiving into something extra special. Grizzly Gramps and Gran, Uncle Wilbur, Aunt Min, and Cousin Fred will be coming over for dinner. I thought we could put on a show for them.”

“A show?” said Sister, looking excited. She loved putting on a show. “What kind of show?”

”I thought the story of the first Thanksgiving would be appropriate,” said Mama. “It could tell all about how the Pilgrims and the Native Bears celebrated the first Thanksgiving together hundreds of years ago.”

“Neat!” said Sister. “Will we have costumes?”

"Of course," said Mama. "We can make them ourselves. I have lots of old fabric we can use. But we'll need feathers for the Native Bears' headdresses."

"Squanto dropped lots of tail feathers," said Sister. "They're perfect! I've been saving them."

She ran upstairs to get her collection of turkey tail feathers. She brought them down to Mama's sewing room. Mama had the *P* book from the Bear Encyclopedia open to *Pilgrims* so she could see what their clothes looked like.

"You're right, dear," said Mama, taking the feathers. "These are perfect. But do you know what else we'll need?"

Sister shook her head.

"We'll need a script for the play," said Mama. "Why don't you write one?"

"Me?"

"Certainly," said Mama, getting out her fabric and spreading it out. "You know the story of the first Thanksgiving, don't you?"

"I guess so," said Sister. She had heard about it in school over and over again every November. She should know it pretty well by now.

"Well, there you are," mumbled Mama, her mouth full of pins as she started work.

So, Sister got out a pad of paper and a pencil and set to work. It was hard. She had never written a play before. She asked Brother for help. Sister wrote the script, and Brother copied the parts for each player. Sister was so busy working on the play that she forgot all about Squanto the turkey for a while.

When Thanksgiving Day finally arrived, everything was ready. The script was written and copied, Mama had sewn beautiful Pilgrim and Native Bear costumes, and the tree house was full of the wonderful smells of Thanksgiving dinner.

Around two o'clock, Grizzly Gramps and Gran, Uncle Wilbur, Aunt Min, and Cousin Fred arrived. Sister and Brother grabbed Fred and took him up to their room to rehearse. Fred had a part in the play too.

An hour later, just before dinnertime, Sister made an appearance on the landing of the stairs. She was dressed as a Pilgrim maiden.

"May I have your attention, please?" she called.

The grown-ups all turned toward her. "Oh, isn't she darling!" said Aunt Min. Sister did look very cute in her Pilgrim maiden hat.

"We will now present *The Story of the First Thanksgiving!*" she announced. The grown-ups all applauded and found their seats to watch the play.

The Pilgrims lived in the Old Country. They wanted to worship God in the way they believed was right. But the rulers of the Old Country would not let them do this. The Pilgrims decided to leave their home and seek a new land where they could worship in freedom.

I am a Pilgrim. I am going on a dangerous journey.
Yes, we are going on a dangerous journey on a ship named the *Mayflower*.
We will try to find the New World.
But we are scared! We've never been on the ocean!
But we are willing to try.
MAYFLOWER

So they went off to find the New World. But it was bad. They got seasick. But one morning they spotted land.

Hurray! Hurray! Now we can build our new homes.

After going to shore, they found a good place to live. They called it Plymouth.

They gave thanks to God for bringing them safely to the new land. Then they got to work building houses for their village. Finally it was finished. Everyone had a home.

Look, who is that coming into the village? It is a Native Bear. I hope he is friendly!

PLYMOUTH ROCK

ME, SQUANTO!
He speaks English! What a miracle!
Squanto was friendly. He helped the Pilgrims grow more food. He showed them how to plant corn. Without Squanto, they would have starved.

Now, let's harvest our crops and have a Thanksgiving feast!
That's a great idea!
And so they did. Squanto came to the feast too. They all bowed their heads and gave thanks to God for leading them to their new home where they could live in peace and freedom. And then they ate and ate and ate!

All the grown-ups clapped and stamped and whistled. It was a big hit! Aunt Min wiped her eyes. "They're all so darling!" she sniffed.

Mama rang a bell in the doorway. "Dinnertime!" she called.

"Yea!" cried the cubs as they ran for the dining room. But then, Sister stopped short.

"Oh, no!" she said. "What about my turkey, Squanto? I forgot all about him! What happened to Squanto?"

"Don't worry, Sister," said Papa, leading her to the window. "Squanto is safe and sound. I decided that turkeys do make good pets after all!"

And there, in his own brand-new pen in the Bears' own backyard, was Squanto. His tail was spread proudly, and he looked very pleased with himself.

"Oh, Squanto!" said Sister, very happy. "Welcome to your new home!"

The Bear family all gathered around the dining table. Everything was just as Papa had imagined it—two kinds of potatoes, stuffing and gravy, corn on the cob and corn muffins, green beans, pumpkin pie with whipped cream, and ice cream too. But, in the center of the table, instead of a roast turkey, there was a magnificent honey-baked salmon.

"MMM-*MMM*!" said all the bears.

Then it was time to say grace. The Bear family held hands and bowed their heads. Grizzly Gramps, as the eldest of the clan, said the prayer.

"Dear Lord, we give thanks for all your blessings—for this great feast that you have provided, for the warm homes that give us shelter, for the love of our family that surrounds us today, and for all the beauties of the earth that you in your great love and wisdom have created. Amen!"

"Amen!" everyone said, picking up their knives and forks.

But Sister had something to add.
"And I am especially thankful for my wonderful new pet, Squanto the turkey!"

"AMEN!" everyone said again. And they all laughed.

"Men!" echoed Honey as they dug into that delicious food like a family of hungry bears.

The Berenstain Bears® and the Joy of Giving

written by Jan and Mike Berenstain

ZONDERkidz

It was the week before Christmas, and all over Bear Country everyone was busy getting ready for the big day. They were Christmas shopping and Christmas decorating and Christmas *everything*.

Down at the Chapel in the Woods, the cubs of Bear Country were busy getting ready for their Christmas Eve play.

It was *The Story of the First Christmas,* and Brother and Sister had an important role. They were to be the camel of the three wise bears. Sister was the front end of the camel, and Brother brought up the rear. They thought it was the best costume ever.

Missus Ursula, their Sunday school teacher, was directing. "All right, Wise Bears," she called, "enter, stage right!"

The three wise bears came on stage. They carried gifts and wore long robes, crowns, and fake beards. They followed the Christmas star made of foil-covered cardboard that hung above the stage. The First Wise Bear was played by Sammy Bruno who had a loose front tooth that made him a little hard to understand.

"A thtar! A thtar!" he cried. "I thee a thtar!"

Missus Ursula sighed. "Okay, camel," she called. "You're on!"

Sister and Brother followed the three wise bears. But it was hard to see out of the costume, and Sister accidentally knocked over a palm tree. The three wise bears tripped, going down in a tangle.

“Oh, dear! Oh, dear!” said Missus Ursula. “Will we ever be ready?”

“Sorry, Missus Ursula,” said Sister, poking her head out. “It’s hard to see in there.”

“I’ll need to make your peepholes bigger,” said Missus Ursula. “That’s enough for today, cubs. It’s time to go home.”

The cubs took off their costumes and went into the chilly evening air.

"Brrr!" shivered Sister. "It's beginning to feel a lot like Christmas!"

"Yeah," agreed Brother, "and looking that way, too."

The whole neighborhood was decorated for Christmas. Sister and Brother walked home in the soft glow of many colored lights.

The next day, the Bear family went shopping. It was time for Brother and Sister to pick out a few special gifts. This year they had two crisp ten-dollar bills from Grizzly Gramps and Gran to spend on others.

Of course, Brother and Sister hoped they would have some money left for themselves. Sister was saving for a brand-new Bearbie doll, and Brother wanted a special rubber band-powered model airplane.

Papa and Honey helped Brother do his shopping while Mama went with Sister. Brother picked out a Bearbie doll outfit that he found on sale for Sister, and Sister bought a small airplane model for Brother. Each cost just a few dollars.

Mama and Papa thought that maybe each cub should have spent more money on one another.

"What about the joy of giving?" whispered Mama to Papa. "It seems Brother and Sister only care about the joy of getting."

"True," agreed Papa, "but let's not interfere. They'll learn about the joy of giving for themselves."

Over the next few days, Christmas excitement in Bear Country grew and grew. Brother and Sister could hardly wait. They were going to be a camel and get lots of presents too.

Play rehearsals went well. Sister could see better out of the bigger peepholes, and everyone knew their lines. But it was still a little hard to understand Sammy Bruin.

When Christmas Eve finally arrived, practically everyone in Bear Country jammed the Chapel in the Woods to see the cubs perform. A hush fell as the curtain opened and the play began.

First, the angel Gabriel came to Mary telling her that she would give birth to Jesus.

Then Joseph and Mary journeyed to Bethlehem where the innkeeper gave them shelter in a stable.

There, Mary gave birth to a tiny baby who was laid in a manger.

An angel of the Lord appeared to the shepherds, sharing the good news of Jesus' birth so they could go and worship the newborn King.

Finally, the three wise bears and their faithful camel trooped on stage. The foil-covered Christmas star hung high above the stable, sparkling in the spotlight.

"A star! A star! I see a star!" Sammy said clearly. His lose tooth had come out backstage.

The three wise bears kneeled before Mary, Joseph, and Jesus. The shepherds and the angel joined them.

Everyone bowed low before the tender baby. The three wise bears opened their treasures and gave Jesus their precious gifts.

The audience grew very still. Then someone in the back began to softly sing.

Silent night, Holy night,
All is calm, all is bright...

And the rest of the audience joined in near the end:

Sleep in heavenly peace,
Sleep in heavenly peace.

Peeking out of the camel costume, tears came to Sister's and Brother's eyes. It seemed they had never understood the joy of giving until that moment. All the gifts of all the Christmases of all the years went back to those first gifts given to the tiny baby long ago.

The Christmas Eve play was over, and the audience cheered. Everyone felt the true spirit of Christmas had been with them that night.

On Christmas morning, Brother and Sister led the family downstairs, bright and early. But instead of heading to their own piles of presents, they went to their gifts for each other.

"Merry Christmas!" they said, holding out their presents.

"From one end of the camel to the other," said Brother.

"Thanks!" laughed Sister. "You're a first-rate backup."

Brother and Sister were delighted with their gifts and gave each other big bear hugs. Honey opened her presents, and Brother and Sister joined in. In the back of their minds, though, they were still thinking about the money they had left over from their shopping trip.

Later that morning, the family went to the Chapel in the Woods for the Christmas Day service. A light snow covered the ground, and all of Bear Country glistened in the sun.

On the way, Sister and Brother noticed a group of bears playing Christmas carols. They were collecting money for the needy in a big black pot. Brother and Sister looked at each other, dug into their pockets, and dropped all of their money into the pot.

Mama and Papa smiled with pride.

"You know what the Good Book says," Mama told them. "'It is more blessed to give than to receive.'"

"We know," said Brother. "We receive an awful lot, so it's time we gave some of it back."

"Look!" said Sister, feeling in her pocket. "I still have a quarter."

Honey reached for it, and Sister put it in her hand.

Then little Honey, holding onto Papa, toddled over to the big black pot and dropped the quarter in. The bears playing music paused.

"Merry Christmas!" they all said.

"Merry Christmas!" answered the Bear family.

The Berenstain Bears®

God Bless Our Home

Activities and Questions from Brother and Sister Bear

Talk about it:

1. Describe the Bear Family tree house. Name the rooms. Is it about the same as your home? How is it the same? How is it different?

2. What happens that makes the Bear Family think their tree house might be getting too small? Why don't Brother and Sister really want to move?

3. How does the Bear Family work together to solve their problem? Talk about ways that you and your family have worked together to solve a problem or issue.

Get out and do it:

1. Help mom and dad make some room around your home. Clean your room and set aside old toys that can be donated to a homeless shelter or the church nursery.

2. Make a "God Bless Our Home" sampler for your family or someone else. If you know how to stitch one, ask for help to get the supplies you need and make one for your wall. Or you can use art and craft supplies such as cardboard, macaroni or yarn, glue, markers, and other decorations to design a poster with the words.

The Berenstain Bears®

PLAY a GOOD GAME

Activities and Questions from Brother and Sister Bear

Talk about it:

1. Do you think Brother Bear played fair? What could he have done differently to please God?

2. How do you feel when someone else does not play fair?

Get out and do it:

1. Play a team game with your friends: tag, soccer, red rover, or baseball.

2. Design a team logo for a sports team, school, club, or church group.

3. The Steamrollers is a good name for Too-Tall's team. It fits how they play. Come up with a team name that fits how you play a game of your choice.

The Berenstain Bears®

Activities and Questions from Brother and Sister Bear

Talk about it:

1. How does the Bear family feel about the Bogg brothers? Do you think they are easy to like?

2. How did the Bear family show their love for their neighbors?

3. How have you shown love for your neighbors?

Get out and do it:

1. Design a fun car with no top.

2. With your family, help a neighbor with a job like yard work.

3. Write three things you can do to help at home.

Activities and Questions from Brother and Sister Bear

Talk about it:

1. What types of things did the Cub Club usually do for the Bear community? Does the youth group or Sunday school at your church do any of the same activities and service projects?

2. Why did many of the bears of Bear Country gather at the Chapel in the Woods?

3. Why do you think Brother and Sister are especially interested in helping out during the big rains?

Get out and do it:

1. As a family, get involved in a community or church project. Help collect food items for a food drive or blankets for a blanket collection. Organize a bake sale, and donate the funds to a local charity or to your church's service organization or mission.

2. Getting involved can be as simple as making cards for neighborhood shut-ins or people from your church that are in the hospital or a nursing home. Gather some of your friends, and make cards or write letters that give encouragement and hope to others.

The Berenstain Bears®

JOBS AROUND TOWN

Activities and Questions from Brother and Sister Bear

Talk about it:

1. Why did Brother and Sister Bear decide to go out and look around Bear Country?

2. How do you know if you have found the right job for you? Where does talent and skill come from?

3. List some of the jobs that you think are most important to the community you live in. Are you interested in any of the jobs? Are these any of the same jobs Brother and Sister saw in Bear Country?

Get out and do it:

1. Talk to a pastor or children's minister about their job. Ask what you might be able to do to help them in their job. As a family, choose one of the ideas and work together to help your church leader. This may be as simple as praying for them or something more active like organizing a church-wide project such as a food drive.

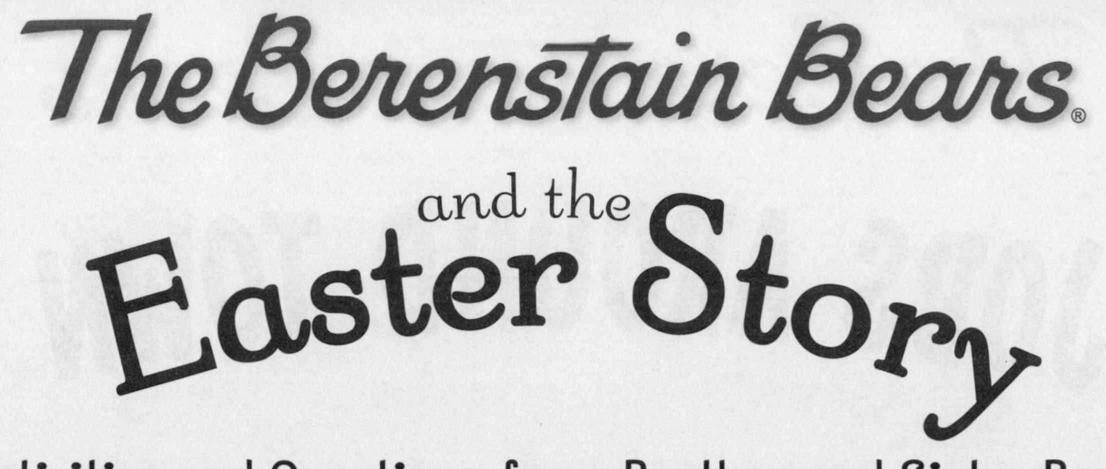

Activities and Questions from Brother and Sister Bear

Talk about it:

1. According to Missus Ursula, there is more to Easter than candy. What does she mean? How does she plan on teaching the Bear cubs this lesson?
2. What types of things did Jesus do for the people while he traveled and preached about his Father's love? Why did some people that heard him teaching get so angry?
3. Talk about why Easter is such a remarkable holy day for Christians.

Get out and do it:

1. Celebrate and share Jesus' love by planning an Easter Egg hunt for some young children in your neighborhood or the preschool class in your Sunday school setting. Put special messages about God's love in plastic eggs and hide them. Have the children gather after the hunt and help them read their messages.
2. Plan and perform an Easter play similar to the one Missus Ursula held in her Sunday school class. If possible, perform for the whole church or the Sunday school parents and students.

Activities and Questions from Brother and Sister Bear

Talk about it:

1. What are you thankful for?

2. What words describe Thanksgiving at your house? Try to use all of your senses and feelings.

3. In what ways is a turkey a good pet? What unusual pet would you like?

Get out and do it:

1. Tell, write, or act out a Thanksgiving story.

2. Draw, color, or make a collage of a turkey and its feathers.

3. Walk like a turkey. Walk like another animal someone names.

Activities and Questions from Brother and Sister Bear

Talk about it:

1. How do you feel when you give a gift to someone? How do you feel when someone gives you a gift?
2. What is the greatest gift that you have ever received? What made it great?
3. Talk about your family's gift-giving traditions and why it is important to give to others?
4. We know that Jesus is God's great gift to the world. Do you think God wants something in return? Did he hold anything back when he gave us his son?

Get out and do it:

1. Design a thank-you card for God. Let him know how much you love and appreciate him and the gift of his son, Jesus.
2. Organize a food drive or coat and blanket drive at your church or school. Choose a group in your community that needs such things and let them know what you are doing. Make posters that let people know who will receive the gift of food or warm clothing. Be sure to include a thank you on the poster.

The Berenstain Bears®

Bind-ups

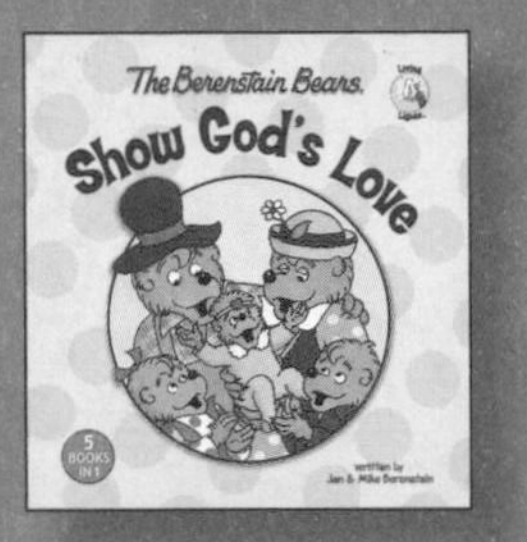

5 Books in 1
9780310720102
$10.99

5 Books in 1
9780310725916
$10.99

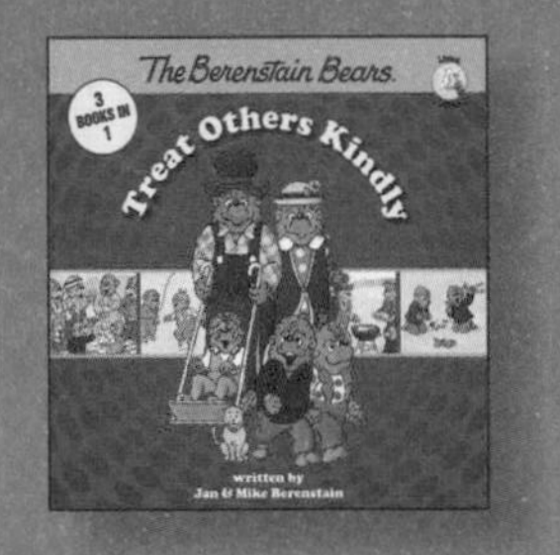

3 Books in 1
9780310734925
$7.99

3 Books in 1
9780310735038
$7.99

Hardcover Titles

9780310719366
$6.99

9780310719373
$6.99

9780310719380
$6.99

9780310719397
$6.99

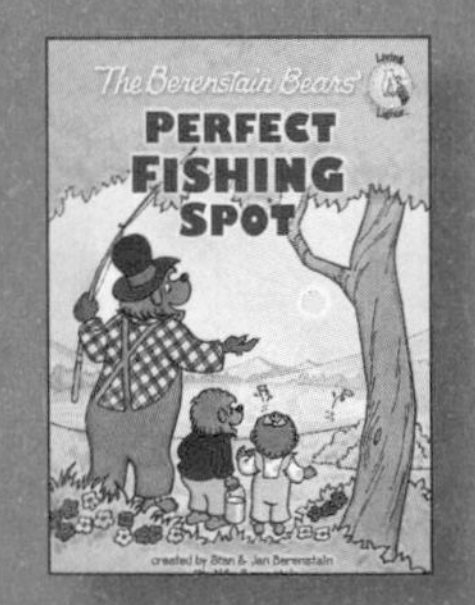

9780310722762
$6.99

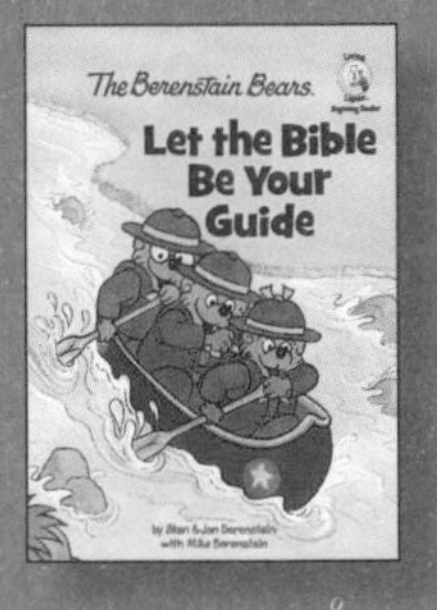

9780310727149
$6.99

9780310722779
$6.99

9780310727132
$6.99